A Note to Parents and Caregivers:

Read-it! Readers are for children who are just starting on the amazing road to reading. These beautiful books support both the acquisition of reading skills and the love of books.

 The PURPLE LEVEL presents basic topics and objects using high frequency words and simple language patterns.

 The RED LEVEL presents familiar topics using common words and repeating sentence patterns.

 The BLUE LEVEL presents new ideas using a larger vocabulary and varied sentence structure.

 The YELLOW LEVEL presents more challenging ideas, a broad vocabulary, and wide variety in sentence structure.

 The GREEN LEVEL presents more complex ideas, an extended vocabulary range, and expanded language structures.

 The ORANGE LEVEL presents a wide range of ideas and concepts using challenging vocabulary and complex language structures.

When sharing a book with your child, read in short stretches, pausing often to talk about the pictures. Have your child turn the pages and point to the pictures and familiar words. And be sure to reread favorite stories or parts of stories.

There is no right or wrong way to share books with children. Find time to read with your child, and pass on the legacy of literacy.

Adria F. Klein, Ph.D.
Professor Emeritus
California State University
San Bernardino, California

To Pierre and Ginette, who taught me to love books

First American edition published in 2005 by
Picture Window Books
5115 Excelsior Boulevard
Suite 232
Minneapolis, MN 55416
877-845-8392
www.picturewindowbooks.com

First published in Canada in 1999 by
Les éditions Héritage inc.
300 Arran Street, Saint Lambert
Quebec, Canada J4R 1K5

Printed in the United States of America.

Library of Congress Cataloging-in-Publication Data
Sarrazin, Marisol, 1965-
Peppy, Patch, and the socks / Marisol Sarrazin.
p. cm. — (Read-it! readers)
Summary: A puppy gets a lesson from his grandfather in how to take care of his teeth, which involves finding, chewing on, and burying various objects.
ISBN 1-4048-1023-4 (hardcover)
[1. Dogs—Fiction. 2. Teeth—Care and hygiene—Fiction. 3. Stories in rhyme.] I. Title.
II. Series.

PZ8.3.S2358Pe 2004
[E]—dc22
2004023779

Peppy, Patch, and the Socks

Written and Illustrated by
Marisol Sarrazin

Special thanks to our advisers for their expertise:

Adria F. Klein, Ph.D.
Professor Emeritus, California State University
San Bernardino, California

Susan Kesselring, M.A.
Literacy Educator
Rosemount - Apple Valley - Eagan (Minnesota) School District

PICTURE WINDOW BOOKS

Hi! My name is Patch.
And this is Thomas, my master.

That's Peppy. I call him Mr. Know-It-All.
He's also my grandpa. He's teaching me
all the things that a little dog should know.

This is normal, since Peppy knows everything. He's a very good teacher. This morning, he told me all about teeth. He cleared his throat and began to speak.

"Patch, little Patch of mine,
you know how important teeth are.
You have to take care of them,
and I'm going to tell you how.

First, choose a sock.

Not too big, not too small,
not too short, not too tall.
Make sure it's wool, and give it a pull.
Cotton's good, too, right from the shoe.

Look in the hamper,
and make those clothes scamper!
Dig to the bottom—
that's where they hide them.

10

Sniff! Sniff!
Choose one carefully.
Sniff it, gnaw it,
then start to paw it.

Then you shake the daylights out of it!

You chew and tickle and tease it.
You bite and pull and squeeze it.

Then you bury it out in the yard!

Patch, little Patch of mine,
that's not all.
Next you find yourself a shoe.

Not too old, not too new,
not all stiff and hard to chew.
Leather's best, and remember, my lad,
forget tennis shoes—they smell too bad.

Look in the closet to find your shoe.
That's where they live, the old and the new.

Take your pick.
Give it a lick or a chew—
that's something all dogs do.

Then you shake the daylights out of it!

You wrestle and gnarl and bite it.
You tussle and snarl and fight it.

Then you bury it out in the yard!

Patch, my little Patch,
after the shoes and socks
come toys.

Not too old, not too new,
a forgotten toy, that'll do!
A favorite thing from the past—
grab on to it and slip out fast.

Up in the attic, there you'll see
a choice of toys for you and me.

You tiptoe with it down the stairs.
You hold it, you fold it,
you grind it to dust.

Then you shake the daylights out of it!

You bend it, you kick it,
you grasp it.
You tear it, you lick it,
you grab on hard.

Then you bury it out in the yard!

That's all for today's lesson."

"Thank you, Grandpa Peppy.
You've taught me all the things
a little dog should know—
a little dog with big teeth!

I hope Thomas will be proud of me now!"

More *Read-it!* Readers

Bright pictures and fun stories help you practice your reading skills. Look for more books at your level.

Clever Cat by Karen Wallace

Flora McQuack by Penny Dolan

Izzie's Idea by Jillian Powell

Naughty Nancy by Anne Cassidy

Parents Do the Weirdest Things! by Louise Tondreau-Levert

Peppy, Patch, and the Socks by Marisol Sarrazin

The Princess and the Frog by Margaret Nash

The Roly-Poly Rice Ball by Penny Dolan

Run! by Sue Ferraby

Sausages! by Anne Adeney

Stickers, Shells, and Snow Globes by Dana Meachen Rau

The Truth About Hansel and Gretel by Karina Law

Willie the Whale by Joy Oades

Looking for a specific title or level? A complete list of *Read-it!* Readers is available on our Web site: *www.picturewindowbooks.com*